The
Great Paint
Problem

The
Great Paint
Problem

by Kimberly Weinberger
Illustrated by Duendes Del Sur

SCHOLASTIC INC.
New York   Toronto   London   Auckland   Sydney
Mexico City   New Delhi   Hong Kong

Chapter One
THE CONTEST

"Kisha's paints are gone!" cried Casey the cat. "All of her colors are gone!"

"Gone, you say?" asked CJ the frog. "Sounds like a mystery. Edison, where's my notebook? I must begin a search!"

CJ's best friend, Edison the firefly, rolled his eyes. "Speaking of mysteries," he groaned. "Casey, how did you find our Secret Clubhouse?"

"Oh, everyone knows where it is," said Casey. "And as for the missing paints, there is no mystery. Kisha let me borrow them."

Then Casey lowered his head.

"I wanted to paint my tail," he said. "But I forgot to bring the paints inside when I was finished. Then it rained and all of Kisha's colors were washed away. And I'm supposed to bring them back by tomorrow afternoon!"

"Oh, boy," said Edison, "you're in trouble now!"

"That's not even the worst part of it," said Casey sadly. "There's an art contest at school in two days. Kisha was planning to paint a picture tomorrow and enter it in the contest. But how can she without any paint?"

CJ's eyes began to shine.

"This sounds like a problem!" he cried. "This could be even better than a mystery."

Edison frowned.

"There is no problem," said Edison. "Why not just tell Kisha what really happened?"

But Casey and CJ didn't seem to hear him.

"CJ," said Casey. "Can you help me buy new paints before Kisha finds out they're missing? They cost fifty cents each."

"Just leave it to us," CJ said with a smile. "CJ the frog is on the job!"

Chapter Two
THE SECRET INGREDIENT

Casey ran home to see how much money he had.

After he had gone, Edison folded his arms and looked at CJ.

"And just how do you plan to help buy those paints?" asked Edison. "We'll never be able to pay for them."

"Never say never, Edison," said CJ.

He searched on a high shelf for the secret clubhouse money box.

He carried it to the table.

"Casey said each of Kisha's paints costs fifty cents," said CJ slowly. "And she had five colors: red, orange, yellow, green, and blue."

"Fifty cents times five colors makes two dollars and fifty cents," said Edison. "That's a lot of money!"

"Let's see how much we've saved," CJ said.
He turned the money jar upside down.
CLINK! CLINK! CLINK!
Three coins fell out.
"Hmmm," said CJ. "Two dimes — ten cents apiece — plus one nickel — or five cents — equals twenty-five cents in all."

"In case you haven't noticed," said Edison, "twenty-five cents is not enough. We still need two dollars and twenty-five cents more."

"You're right," said CJ. "It's time for action!" Edison watched as CJ grabbed a jar.

"All we need to do is find something to sell," CJ said. "And I know just the thing!"

CJ pulled on his tallest boots. He was ready!

"I'm off on a top-secret mission," the frog whispered. "If I'm not back in one hour, send out a search party."

"Oh, good grief!" said Edison.

By the time CJ returned, Casey had come back to the clubhouse, too.

"I only had seventy-five cents," Casey said.

He showed CJ one quarter, four dimes, and ten pennies.

"Great!" said CJ.

"What's so great about it?" Edison asked.
"With our twenty-five cents, we only have
one dollar in all. We still need one dollar and
fifty cents more."

"That's where my idea comes in," said CJ.
"We can use my top-secret recipe!"

CJ showed them a bottle filled with water.

"Water?" said Casey. "What's that for?"

"It's the first step toward buying those paints," said CJ.

Edison and Casey watched as CJ placed a bowl of lemons on the table.

"Water and lemons," said Edison. "Is that some strange recipe for making paint?"

"Not quite," CJ laughed. "We're going to make lemonade! With my family's secret recipe, we'll sell tons of it."

"What's so special about your recipe?" asked Casey.

"Well," CJ said slowly. "I guess I can tell you. But remember — it's a secret!"

He pulled Casey and Edison toward him.

"This ingredient has been guarded by my family for years," CJ whispered.

Casey's eyes grew wide.

"What is it?" he asked.

CJ smiled.

He looked to his left, then to his right.

Finally he said, "It's the juice of one fresh orange."

He pulled a large, round orange from his pocket.

"I picked this one from a tree near the pond," he told them. "It's perfect!"

As he began to peel the orange, CJ turned to Casey.

"Your troubles are over, my friend," he said. "With this orange, we can't miss!"

Chapter Three

AT THE PLAYGROUND

The three friends set up their lemonade stand near the playground.

"There's nothing like a ball game to make you thirsty," said CJ.

Soon they had their first customer.

"Lemonade!" said Frankie. "I'd love some!"

CJ poured his friend a cup.

"That will be ten cents, please," he said.

Edison and Casey watched closely as Frankie drank down the whole cup.

"Hey!" said Frankie. "That's great lemonade! What do you use to make it taste so good?"

"I'm afraid I can't tell you that," said CJ proudly. "It's top-secret information."

Frankie asked for another cup.
And another after that!
Before long, the whole gang had joined them.
Each tried to guess the secret ingredient.
Eleanor thought it was a pineapple.
Pierre was sure it must be a banana.
When nearly all of the lemonade was sold,
the last customer of the day arrived.
"Oh, no!" whispered Casey. "It's Kisha!"

"I'd like one cup, please," Kisha said.
Casey quickly poured Kisha's drink.
But he would not take her dime.
"It's the last cup, anyway," said Casey.
"Here. Take it."
"Thanks!" said Kisha with a smile.
"Oh, and please don't forget to bring my
paints back tomorrow," she added. "I need
them to paint my picture for the contest."

"Don't worry," Casey said nervously. "I'll bring — er — some paints to you tomorrow."

When she had gone, CJ counted their money.

"We sold ten cups of lemonade for ten cents apiece," said CJ. "That makes 10, 20, 30, 40, 50, 60, 70, 80, 90, 100 cents!" They had made one whole dollar selling lemonade!

"That means we have two dollars altogether!" cried CJ.

"We still need fifty cents more," said Casey, shaking his head. "And time is running out!"

Chapter Four

LOST AND FOUND

That night, CJ, Edison, and Casey tried to find a solution to their problem. As the sun came up, CJ heard a knock on his door. He opened it and there was Casey jumping up and down.

"I've got it!" shouted Casey. "I've got it!"

"Well, keep it to yourself," mumbled a sleepy Edison. "Some of us are trying to sleep!"

"But I've got the last fifty cents!" Casey said again.

"How?" asked CJ.

"My tooth fell out last night!" Casey said proudly. "I found seventy-five cents under my pillow this morning! Now I can pay you back your twenty-five cents and still have the last fifty cents we need for the new paints!"

Then Casey hurried off to buy Kisha a new paint set. He got it to her just in time.

The next day, CJ, Edison, and Casey joined all of their friends at the art contest.

Kisha won first prize!

After winning, she found Casey in the crowd. "Casey," she said, "I'm so glad you are here! Thank you for coming to the art contest."

Seeing the smile on Kisha's face, Casey felt terrible inside. He knew he had to tell his friend the truth about what had happened.

Casey stared at the ground as he told Kisha the whole story.

"I'm sorry," he said quietly. "I thought you'd be angry. Your paints were ruined because of me."

"I'm sorry, too," CJ said. "After all, it was my idea to raise the money and buy new paints."

"Ruining the paints was an accident," said Kisha. "There was no reason to keep it a secret. It's always better to tell the truth."

"Not to mention a lot less work," Edison grumbled.

Then Kisha smiled.

"You'll never guess what the prize was for first place," said Kisha.

"What?" asked Casey.

"A brand new set of paints!" Kisha said with a grin. "I can't wait to get started on my new picture for next week's contest."

"What are you going to paint?" CJ asked.

"Oh, it's a secret!," Kisha answered. "But I can tell you it will have lots of colors!"

There's No Stopping a Kid With a JumpStart!

S C H O L A S T I C

JumpStart™ Readers

JumpStart Learning System is tested by kids, endorsed by teachers, approved by parents!

Scholastic, the most trusted name in learning, and JumpStart, the # 1 educational software for children,* have united to create a fresh new series of educational JumpStart Readers. Children will learn to read as they are introduced to money-counting skills in a fun and engaging way. Each JumpStart Reader adventure is based on the JumpStart characters children know and love.

The JumpStart Learning System brings to life a world where children enjoy reading. It's a place where learning means *fun*!

JumpStart Readers grow with children as *their* reading skills grow!

Collect all of the JumpStart Readers:

Pre-K:	*Eleanor's Enormous Ears* *Lost and Found in JumpStart Town*
Kindergarten:	*Hopsalot's Garden* *Rain, Rain, Go Away*
1st Grade:	*A Wild Weather Day* *Just in Time!*
2nd Grade:	*The Great Paint Problem* *CJ and the Mysterious Map*

*PC Data Interactive, January1995–June1999, aggregate dollar and unit sales.

SCHOLASTIC INC.

Knowledge Adventure

$3.99 US
$4.99 CAN

ISBN 0-439-20321-X

EAN

9 780439 203210

50399

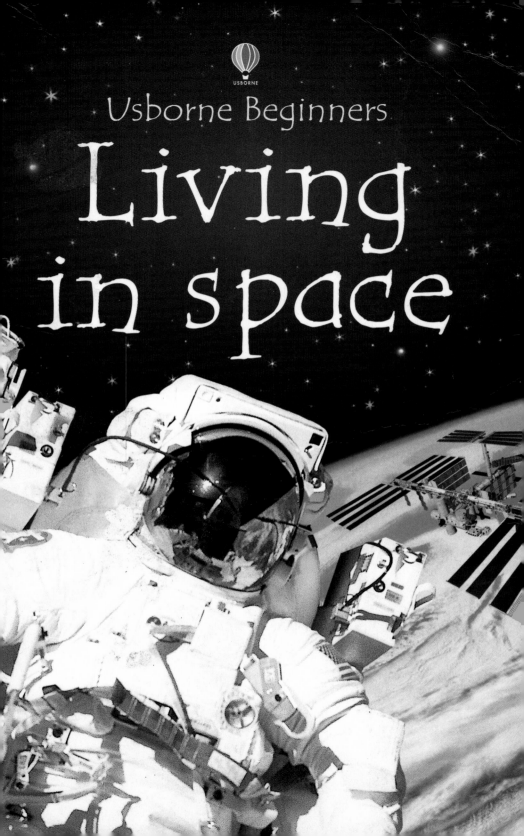

Usborne Beginners

Living in space